PARTY GIRLS

Sunny's Dream Team

PARTY GIRLS

Sunny's Dream Team

Jennie Walters

illustrated by Jessie Eckel

Hodder
Children's
Books

a division of Hodder Headline Limited

For Laura Fisher

FACT FILE: SUNNY

Full name: Sunanda Kumar
Nicknames: Sunny, Nanda
Family: Mum Shaila, dad Anil,
  older brothers Arjun and Sachin,
  younger sister Anisha
Star sign: Virgo
Hair: black
Eyes: brown
Likes: reading, playing on the computer,
  long holidays, Mum's cooking, toffee ice cream
Dislikes: games, being late
Favourite thing in wardrobe: my
  white beaded top
Favourite food: chicken tikka
Favourite pizza topping: chilli and
  mushroom
Ambition: work with computers? Be a
  journalist?

'How about this one?' Jess said, shooting a photo across the carpet to Sunny. 'Mum took it when we were in the middle of our dance routine. Don't you think we look cool?'

Sunny had invited her five best friends – Jess, Michelle, Caz, Lauren and Nikki – round for a sleepover that Saturday night, while her two older brothers were away for the weekend and there was lots of room to do girly things. Jess had arrived with a sheaf of photos taken at the disco she'd given a couple of weeks before with her twin brother Matt to celebrate their joint birth-day. Now everyone was poring eagerly over the pictures, up in the loft room at the top of Sunny's house. It couldn't be used as a proper bedroom because you had to climb up a ladder to reach it, but it was a great place for sleepovers! There was a big sofabed and a couple of blow-up mattresses, so all Sunny's friends could stay over. They had to squash up together, but nobody minded that.

'Hey, we look wicked!' Sunny said, checking the picture carefully. There they all were, dressed up in their party gear and dancing in time. More or less in time, anyway – everyone's arms were up in the air except for Sunny's. She wasn't looking too bad, though: that leopard-print top she'd bought for the disco was fab. OK, it might not have been as glitzy as Jess's red boob tube or Michelle's strappy dress, but she wouldn't have felt confident wearing anything like that – and her mum and dad would have had a fit!

'Don't sound so surprised,' Jess said, shuffling through the rest of the photographs to find her favourites. 'Here, Caz – this is a great one of you and Lauren together, out on the balcony.'

'That was such a good evening,' Sunny sighed, still gazing at the photo. 'My legs were really stiff the next day from all that dancing.'

'Sunny! You must be so unfit!' Nikki exclaimed. 'You know what would do you good, don't you? Some regular exercise and—'

'No, Niks!' Sunny said, passing her the photograph. 'For the last time, I am *not* interested in joining your girls' footie team! I can't think of anything I'd like to do less with my Saturday mornings.'

'But it'll be a laugh,' Nikki wheedled, trying to persuade her, 'and it's only for an hour and a half. Jess is coming along, so why don't you give it a go too? We only need one more person to make up a team. Come on, Sunny – *please!*'

'Look, I'm sorry, Nikki,' Sunny said firmly. 'If it was anything else, I'd try to help you out, but I'm useless at football and I hate it. You'll have to find somebody else.'

'Michelle?' Nikki tried, giving her friend's glossy chestnut hair a tug to get her attention.

'Gerroff!' Michelle growled good-naturedly, tossing her hair back out of reach. 'Come on,

Nikki, you know I have drama on Saturday mornings. We're doing this fantastic new number,' she added, scrambling to her feet. 'Do you want to hear it?'

'Maybe later, when we've put the photos away,' Sunny said hastily. Michelle had a fantastic voice, but once she started singing you couldn't get her to stop. She liked everyone to pay attention, too – no pretending to listen with half an ear while you did something else!

'Caz? Lauren? How about you?' Nikki tried as a last resort.

Lauren looked up. She was sitting cross-legged, surrounded by a big circle of photographs spread out on the floor. 'Nah, sorry, Niks,' she said, wrinkling her nose. 'It's not really my kind of thing either. Jess, can I borrow some of these photos? There's a colour copier at the library and you can get them blown up to A4 size for a pound. I want to put them up round my room.'

'That's a good idea!' Sunny said. Lauren was always rearranging her bedroom and coming up with ideas to make it look different. 'Could you

4

get some copies for me too? I'll give you the money.'

'And me!' Caz added, holding back her long blonde hair with one hand as she leant over the prints to choose her favourites. The others chimed in too, and soon Lauren had so many different orders she had to write down a list.

'You must get a copy of this one, Miche,' Jess said, holding up a photo so Michelle could see. 'It's you and Matt dancing together, when they were picking the best couple. And here you are, getting the prize! D'you remember? He wouldn't kiss you!'

'I didn't want him to, don't worry!' Michelle said, as her friends started giggling. 'Your brother's not exactly Freddie Prinze Junior, is he?' She snatched the photo out of Jess's hands to give it the once-over.

'So you won't be wanting a copy, then?' Lauren asked, her pen poised over the list.

'Oh, go on, then – maybe I will,' Michelle said, trying to sound casual as she flipped the picture back to Jess. 'I can put it up on my pinboard and throw darts at it.'

'Oh yeah?' Jess said, catching Lauren's eye and winking at her. They were all sure that Michelle secretly fancied Matt. She usually blushed whenever she saw him. And whenever the DJ at the disco had told everyone to get into couples, somehow she'd always ended up dancing with him.

'What about you, Caz?' Nikki asked, prodding Caz's denim-covered leg.

'Why should *I* want a copy?' Caz said, surprised. 'I'm not the one with a crush on Matt, am I?'

'I don't mean *that*, durr brain!' Nikki retorted. 'I'm asking if you want to come and join our footie team.'

'I don't know,' Caz said doubtfully. 'I'm not that keen, to be honest. Running around in the mud isn't my idea of fun.'

'But there isn't any mud!' Nikki said. 'Summer's here – we haven't had any rain for ages.' She looked up at the square of blue sky framed by the loft window. 'And think how fit you'll get! My dad's going to help us with training, and he's got loads of good warm-up exercises. They're great for toning your legs.'

Now that's a clever thing to say, Sunny thought, watching Caz begin to waver. She'd got it into her head that her legs were fat, though nobody else could see the problem.

'Kicking a ball really firms up your muscles,' Nikki went on persuasively. She pushed up one leg of her tracksuit trousers and grabbed a handful of calf. 'Here – feel this!'

'It's OK, I'll take your word for it,' Caz giggled, pushing her away. 'Just tell me, I wouldn't have to play in shorts, would I?'

'You don't have to,' Nikki reassured her. 'Trackies like these are fine. You might get a bit hot, though. And if you wear shorts, your legs will get a great tan. Oh, come on, Caz – just try one session. I bet you'll love it!'

'OK, then,' Caz decided. 'I'll come along next week and give it a go. I'm not promising anything, though.'

'Brilliant!' Nikki smiled, giving her a high five. 'You won't regret it!'

Just then, a plaintive voice floated up from below. 'Mum says tea's ready. You've got to come downstairs.'

7

Sunny looked down through the open trap-door into the heart-shaped face of her five-year-old sister, Anisha. Whenever she had friends over, Anisha wouldn't leave them alone and she usually ended up getting banished downstairs. She was always trying to join in with whatever the 'big girls' were doing and then whingeing because they didn't pay her enough attention.

'Your little sister is so cute,' Caz whispered to Sunny as they started climbing down the ladder.

'Sometimes,' Sunny muttered back. 'She can be a right pain too. Remember, you don't know her like we do.'

Sunny, Lauren, Michelle, Nikki and Jess had been friends for ages, but Caz was a newcomer. She'd moved into the house next door to Lauren in the Easter holidays (which was how they'd got to know her in the first place), though now it seemed as though she'd always been part of their gang.

'This is great, Mum!' Sunny said, looking at all the food laid out in the kitchen and giving her mother a hug. She heaped her plate with rice and added some spicy chicken strips, deciding that her mother was definitely the best cook in the world.

'Do you want some of this chicken?' she asked Michelle, who was staring at the dishes of curry doubtfully. 'It's not too hot.'

Michelle was a real fusspot when it came to food. 'OK,' she said suspiciously, holding out her plate. 'Thanks. Is there any tomato ketchup?'

Sunny's mum laughed and opened the fridge. 'Here you are,' she said, passing the squeezy bottle over. 'Look, why don't you roll the meat up in a chapatti with some salad?'

'Oh, yeah – a chicken wrap,' Michelle said, looking happier. 'I like those.'

Sunny caught her mother's eye and they smiled at each other.

There was silence for a while after the girls had settled down to eat. Anisha had made a huge fuss, as usual, about sitting at the top of the table. Sunny could see that Caz was beginning to have second thoughts about her cute little sister.

And then Caz said, in between mouthfuls,

'Talking of photos, Sunny – that magazine hasn't sent yours back, I suppose? Remember, the ones you took at *my* party? I'd love to get a copy of that picture Natalie took. You know, all of us together outside the shed?'

Sunny shook her head. 'No, not yet,' she said briefly, feeling a pang of disappointment.

About six weeks before, she'd entered a magazine competition. You had to write about the best party you'd ever been to, so she'd described the surprise party they'd thrown for Caz's birthday and sent along a few photos she'd taken with a disposable camera. Caz had gone out for the day and, while she was away, they'd cleared out the big shed at the bottom of her garden and decorated it with a moon and stars theme. And then, after they'd eaten and talked and played some games, Caz's stepsister Natalie had made a camp fire, and they'd sat around it for ages, toasting marshmallows and talking some more. That was what had made the party so special, she'd written: they'd hardly known Caz before then, but that magic evening had helped turn them all into best friends.

'You never know – maybe they're keeping the pictures because I've won,' Sunny added, tearing off a piece of soft, warm chapatti.

'Nice try, but I don't think so,' Jess snorted. 'You'd have heard by now, wouldn't you?'

When Sunny had first told the others about her entry, they'd been really excited. Especially when they'd found out that the top prize was for the winner *and* a group of her friends. They would be modelling clothes for a photo shoot and staying overnight in some posh London hotel. Sunny wasn't expecting to win that, of course, but there were five runner-up prizes too: thirty-pound vouchers to spend at Glitterbug, the cool accessories shop. There was a branch in their local shopping centre, and she

always spent ages browsing through the sparkling jewellery, bags and belts. Secretly, she did think maybe one of those thirty-pound vouchers might end up plopping through her letterbox. She'd tried hard to make her writing punchy and fun, and the photos had come out really well – particularly the shot of them all sitting round the fire.

But the weeks had gone by without a word from *Girlgroove* magazine, and everyone seemed to have accepted that Sunny hadn't got anywhere with her entry.

There was still a tiny flicker of hope inside her, though, that refused to die down. After all, Sunny reasoned, *somebody* had to win, didn't they? And this time, why shouldn't it be her?

'I'm not holding your hand! Go away! I hate you!'

Anisha struggled furiously to tear her clenched fist out of Sunny's grip. Her face was still wet with tears from the tantrum she'd thrown earlier that morning. Sunny had accidentally eaten the last Weetabix, and that had been enough to send Anisha into orbit. It had taken so long trying to calm her down and get her out of the house that now everyone was going to be late.

'You *have* to hold my hand when we're crossing the road,' Sunny hissed, bending down so she was on a level with Anisha. 'If you don't, you could run out and get knocked down by a car.'

'If I get hit by a car, *you'll* be in trouble,' Anisha

retorted. She looked at the stream of traffic rushing past them, as if wondering whether being knocked down would be worth it if Sunny got the blame.

Sunny's father took her and Anisha and the two boys to school every morning on his way to work, and her mum picked them up in the afternoon. The boys always waited in the car while Sunny crossed Anisha over the road to school. It wasn't fair, she thought crossly to herself. Why couldn't Sachin and Arjun take their turn? Just because she was a girl, it didn't mean she had to look after her little sister the whole time.

'We'd better hurry,' her father said, after Sunny had run back to the car and they were setting off again on the next part of the school run. By the time they'd dropped off the boys and arrived at Greenside School, Sunny was flustered and cross. She hated being late; it got the whole day off to a bad start. Her class was having a computer studies lesson first thing, too, and she usually helped their teacher, Miss Gibson, set up the program and make sure it was running properly.

Sunny knew a lot about computers; they'd had one at home for a few years now, mainly to keep in touch with all the family in Bombay. She e-mailed her cousins on their birthdays and festivals, and she was beginning use the Internet for looking things up, too. There were so many cool websites to visit (though her parents insisted on checking them first), and she could print out brilliant pictures and graphics for her school projects. She couldn't wait for her friends to get connected so they could all e-mail each other.

By the time Sunny made it to her classroom Miss Gibson was just about to take the register. 'Ah, Sunny, there you are,' she said, looking up over her glasses. 'Sit down as quickly as you can, please.'

Sunny slid into the nearest chair and gave Jess and Nikki a hurried smile. Caz, Lauren and Michelle were all in another class, along with Jess's brother Matt. She took a couple of books out of her bag and tried to catch her breath.

'What happened to you?' Jess asked, when they'd filed over to the computer room after assembly and were sitting in their groups for that lesson's project.

'Anisha was playing up again,' Sunny replied through gritted teeth. 'One day I'm going to—'

'Stop talking, please!' Miss Gibson called from the corner. 'Really, Sunanda – this isn't like you! Settle down and get on with your work right now.'

'Sorry, Miss,' Sunny muttered, feeling her cheeks burn. She started to turn the pages of the History book in front of them on the table. The class was putting together a newspaper from Tudor times. Each group had to write a report on a different topic which Miss Gibson would help them turn into one document and jazz up with fancy formats and headings. Sunny's group – Jess, Kayleigh Brown, Joseph Taylor, Murray Carter and herself – had to imagine they'd just come back from a trip overseas on the *Golden Hinde*.

'I'm going to be captain of this stupid ship,' Murray announced importantly. 'Let's say there was a mutiny and I threw all the crew over-board.'

Kayleigh tittered.

'So you sailed it back on your own, I suppose,' Jess said sarcastically. 'Murray Carter, Superhero.'

'Come on,' Sunny said, growing even more impatient and cross. 'It'll be our turn on the computer soon. What are we going to write? We have to put in something historical.' She took out a piece of paper, ready to make notes.

'Let's describe what it was like on board,' Joseph suggested, flicking over a page. 'You know, the food and everything. Look, here – where it says about the sailors getting scurvy and eating ship's biscuits.'

'Ooh, I'll have some of those!' Jess said. 'Custard creams or chocolate digestives?'

Murray let out a guf-faw at this and Kayleigh started giggling.

Sunny saw Miss Gibson look over at their table and

frown. 'For goodness' sake, Jess! Can't you take anything seriously?' she hissed furiously at her friend. 'You're going to get us all into trouble!'

Miss Gibson was one of the nicest teachers in the school, and Sunny hated being in her bad books. Besides, this was a really interesting project and she wanted to make a good job of it. Why did Jess have to spoil everything by acting like an idiot? She could be a real laugh sometimes, but there was a time and a place for everything.

Jess shot her an angry look. 'So who rattled your cage?' she flashed back, the colour rising in her cheeks. 'Sorry, I'm sure.'

'Right, Jess's group,' Miss Gibson announced. 'As you're so busy talking, you've obviously decided what to put in your report. Come over here and write it up on the computer. Sunny, you can start off.'

Jess wouldn't look at Sunny as their group straggled over to the computer table, but started whispering to Kayleigh instead. Miss Gibson had them all under her eagle eye and Sunny didn't dare risk another telling-off, so she settled herself in the chair and prepared to type.

'Shall I begin with something about the ship's rations, then?' she asked, glancing at Jess and giving her a half smile, to signal that she was sorry she'd been so snappy.

Jess wasn't having any of it. 'Don't look at me,' she retorted sniffily. 'You're the boffin round here – write what you like.'

'But we're all meant to be doing this together!' Sunny said, upset.

Jess had already turned away, though, and was pretending to concentrate on the History book. She didn't speak to Sunny for the rest of that lesson or the next two. And as soon as it was time for break, she headed straight outside. By the time Sunny had arrived in the playground, Jess was arm in arm with Michelle and very obviously avoiding her. Michelle lived a couple of doors away from Jess, and they often went round together. Nikki had run off to join in a football game with the boys, so Sunny was left feeling like a lemon on her own.

'Hi, there! What's the matter?' Lauren asked, strolling over with Caz. 'You look fed up.'

'Oh, nothing really,' Sunny shrugged, not

wanting to look as though she cared too much. 'You know – Mondays.'

'We had a blast on Saturday, didn't we?' Caz said, smiling at her. 'It was so funny when you and Jess had that WWF wrestling competition in your sleeping bags! I was laughing so much it hurt.'

Sunny couldn't help glancing over at Jess, on the other side of the playground by now. She chewed her lip anxiously.

'What's the matter?' Lauren asked, not missing a trick. 'Have you two fallen out?'

Sunny nodded miserably. 'Look, I like Jess and I know she's really funny and everything,' she burst out, 'but sometimes she doesn't know when to stop! We were meant to be doing this project together and she was just mucking around and being stupid.'

'Never mind,' Caz said, giving her a comforting hug. 'You know what Jess is like. She'll have got over it by this afternoon, you'll see. Maybe you should try and make up with her after school.'

'Maybe,' Sunny said doubtfully. She'd already

tried to make up with Jess and had it thrown back in her face. It was Jess's turn now. And if she didn't come and say she was sorry, this could be the end of a beautiful friendship!

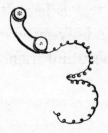

'Come on, Mum! Open the door!' Sunny said impatiently as her mother fumbled with her keys on the doorstep that afternoon. Her brothers were still taking their cricket kit out of the car and Anisha was busy inspecting a ladybird in the front garden, but Sunny just wanted to get inside as quickly as possible. She'd had such a horrible day, all she wanted to do was go up to her room, change out of her school clothes and try and forget everything that had happened.

'Wait a second, for goodness' sake,' her mother scolded mildly. 'Stop rushing me!'

At last she managed to open the door. Sunny dumped her school bag under the hall table and headed straight upstairs. By the time she'd changed into jeans and a sloppy T-shirt and flopped on her bed for half an hour with a magazine, she was beginning to feel better. But she still didn't really feel like emerging from her comfy cocoon when her mother called up the stairs, 'Sunanda! Phone for you.'

Maybe it was Jess, though, ringing to make the peace. Sunny swung her legs off the bed and thundered down the stairs, feeling slightly nervous.

'Hello?' she gasped into the receiver, out of breath.

'Is that Sunanda Kumar?' said a chirpy voice on the other end of the line.

'Yes, that's right. It is,' Sunny said, wondering what was coming next. She could feel her heart thumping in her chest. Perhaps Nikki was right – she really ought to take some more exercise.

'Well, this is Anna Nicholson,' the voice went on importantly, 'and I'm ringing from *Girlgroove* magazine. Are you sitting down? I've got some very exciting news to tell you!'

'Wha-what d'you mean?' Sunny stammered, suddenly feeling her knees turn to jelly. She sank into the hall chair next to the phone, her heart pounding even harder now. Surely this call couldn't be about the competition, could it?

It was.

'Remember the competition you entered a few weeks ago?' Anna Nicholson asked next. 'Where you had to describe your best ever party? And you sent us that lovely piece about the surprise party you threw for your new friend?'

'Yes, that's right,' Sunny whispered, feeling her heart leap into her throat.

'Well . . . you've won!' Anna Nicholson finished triumphantly.

For a moment, Sunny couldn't think of anything to say. She could hear her mother clattering about in the kitchen, and the soundtrack from Anisha's video floating out through the open living-room door – but it was as though she'd suddenly been transported to another universe. Time seemed to have frozen into this one incredible, exciting, wonderful moment.

'Sunanda? Are you still there?'

'Yes, I'm here,' Sunny said slowly. 'That's fantastic! I can't believe it!'

Her entry had actually won a prize, out of all the

hundreds or even thousands that must have been sent in! She could go round Glitterbug with some money in her pocket for a change. Thirty pounds! That would buy her a bag, and one of those brilliant sparkly belts, and a couple of hair slides, or—

Anna Nicholson was saying something else. '. . . a letter in the post, but we wanted to make sure that you and your friends are free next Saturday. It is rather short notice, I'm afraid, but our editor's been away and we couldn't confirm the details until she came back.'

'Next Saturday?' Sunny repeated, puzzled. Did she have to go shopping on one particular day? That was a bit odd, wasn't it?

'That's right,' Ms Nicholson said. 'Not this one

coming up, but the next. That's when we've scheduled your photo shoot, and your overnight stay in the hotel. You are available then, I hope?'

Sunny's head swam. She wasn't a runner-up. She hadn't won a thirty-pound voucher. She'd won the top prize! The makeovers, and everything else! This was too much to take in all at once – it was all she could do to stay sitting upright on the chair.

'Yes,' she said, in a faraway voice. 'I'm sure I'm free.'

'Good!' Anna Nicholson said, and Sunny could tell that she was smiling. 'I'll talk to you again, after you and your parents have read our letter. It should arrive tomorrow, with a bit of luck. Bye for now! I'll look forward to meeting you.'

'Right,' Sunny said faintly, still stunned. 'Goodbye.' Just before she replaced the receiver, she remembered to blurt out, 'And thanks! Thank you very much. This is just amazing!'

A couple of minutes later, Anisha had the shock of her life when Sunny came rushing into the sitting room and swept her off the sofa into a great big hug. 'Yes!' she was shouting, her face wreathed in smiles as she planted a smacker on her sister's cheek. 'I did it! I won!'

'Won what?' Anisha demanded. 'Put me down, you're squashing me! What did you win? I want it!'

But Sunny was too excited to take any notice. 'Mum!' she yelled, dancing through to the kitchen with Anisha in her arms. 'Listen to this! I've won the *Girlgroove* competition! First prize! I'm going to London, with my friends!'

An hour later, Sunny was still smiling. She sat at the kitchen table with Anisha on her lap, eating a big bowl of ice cream to celebrate and listening to her mother talking excitedly on the phone. As soon as Mrs Kumar had heard the news, she'd insisted on ringing practically everyone she'd ever met to tell them all about her brilliant daughter. Luckily, she was speaking in Hindi. Sunny could only pick up the odd word here and there, so she didn't have to feel too embarrassed about her mother gushing on.

'Are you sure this isn't a wind-up?' her oldest brother Arjun asked, lounging against the counter with his hands in his trouser pockets. 'It wasn't one of your friends fooling around, by any chance?'

For a second, Sunny panicked. That was just the kind of thing Jess might do, particularly given the mood she was in right now. Then she remembered the voice on the phone – there was no way Jess could have sounded like that. 'It's for real, I'm sure of it!' she told her brother. 'And there's a letter in the post, so we'll soon know for certain.'

Arjun doesn't like anyone else having all the attention, she realised, looking at her brother's handsome, sulky face. Both the boys were doing really well at secondary school, and Sunny sometimes felt she'd scream if she had to listen to any more of their triumphs – the matches they'd helped to win, the brilliant marks they'd scored, the music exams they'd passed with distinction. Well, now they'd have to get used to their sister being in the spotlight for a change!

Sachin was much nicer. 'This is great, Nanda!'

he said, looking up at her across the table after he'd finished the article. (Sunny's mother had insisted that she print out several copies so they could all read it.) 'I never knew you could write so well. You're going to be a journalist when you grow up, then, and support the rest of us?'

'You must be joking!' Sunny grinned, putting down her spoon. 'You can look after yourselves.'

Anisha's little fingers snaked out and twined themselves in Sunny's long black hair. 'Can't I come to London with you, Nanda?' she wheedled. 'I want to be in the magazine too. Please let me come!'

'No,' Sunny said firmly. 'Sorry, Anisha, but you're not old enough. This is just for me and my friends. If you're a good girl, though, I'll bring you back a present.'

'I don't want a stupid present,' Anisha said crossly, scrambling off her lap. 'Why can't I go to London? It's not fair!' She flounced out of the kitchen, slamming the door behind her.

'So, what is this great prize?' Arjun asked loftily.

Sunny refused to let him spoil her mood.

'Well, I can't remember everything exactly,' she began, 'and I've lost the magazine with all the details in. But I know we're going to be modelling party clothes for a photo shoot. Our pictures are going to be printed in the magazine! And then they take us out for a meal somewhere and we stay overnight in a hotel and come home the next day.'

'You know Mum and Dad don't like you wearing make-up, though,' Arjun said triumphantly. Managing to think up some drawback had made him look almost pleased.

'Come off it, Arjun!' Sachin protested. 'They won't mind if it's a special occasion! Why can't you just say well done instead of being so miserable? Not jealous, are you?'

'Don't be stupid,' Arjun replied, slouching out of the door. 'You wouldn't catch me poncing around for some stupid magazine. Well done, though, Nanda,' he managed to add as a grudging afterthought. 'I hope you enjoy yourself.'

'Don't worry, I will!' Sunny replied happily, giving Sachin a wink to say thanks. She'd just heard the sound she'd been waiting for: her father's key in the front door. He was the one person she'd managed to ring before her mother had snatched the phone out of her hands, and he'd promised to come home early from work.

She rushed down the hall and threw herself into her father's arms. With her face pressed against his sweet-smelling white shirt, she heard the words that mattered so much more than anything Arjun could say.

'Well done, *beti*! Who's my clever girl, then?'

Sunny sat on the stairs the next morning, waiting for the postman and thinking. Her argument with Jess made everything so much more complicated. She'd been just about to start ringing round the night before to tell her friends the amazing news – when her mother had finally let go of the phone – but then she'd suddenly had second thoughts. How could she invite Jess when they weren't speaking? And did she want her to come along, anyway, after she'd been so mean?

On the other hand, Jess was still one of her best buddies – she couldn't imagine spending such a fantastic day without her. And as soon as she told everyone else about winning the competition, Jess would be sure to find out. The trouble was – if she tried to make up with Sunny then, it would look like she was only doing it to muscle in on the trip to London . . .

Sunny sighed, finally deciding to wait one more day before breaking the news. It would be hard to keep such an exciting secret (she couldn't wait to see her friends' faces when she told them they'd be appearing in *Girlgroove*!), but she had to sort things out with Jess first. If the two of them could make up before Jess heard anything about the prize, then she'd know her friendship was genuine.

The flap of the letterbox and a cascade of letters on to the mat interrupted her thoughts. She tumbled down the last few stairs, scooped up the envelopes and began sorting hurriedly through them. There it was! A white envelope hidden between two brown ones, addressed to  'Miss S Kumar', with the *Girlgroove* logo across the front. Sunny could hardly bring herself to open it. Seeing her amazing prize written down in black and white would make it finally seem real. She felt nervous. What if Anna Nicholson had muddled the entries and she was just a runner-up, after all? What if the judges had changed their minds?

Telling herself not to be so stupid, Sunny quickly tore the envelope open before she could lose her nerve and began to read . . .

'Hey, what's up with you?' Nikki said, waving her hand in front of Sunny's face. 'You nearly walked straight past me!'

'Sorry, Niks,' Sunny said, coming back to reality with a start. 'I've got a lot on my mind at the moment.'

The letter from *Girlgroove* had certainly given her plenty to think about. As her eyes had skimmed over it that morning, one big problem had leapt off the page and cast a shadow over everything else. The situation had become even more complicated, in a way that Sunny could never have imagined . . .

Miss Gibson and a couple of the other teachers had appeared now, so everyone started to queue up in their classes before filing into school. Out of the corner of her eye, Sunny noticed a flash of auburn hair near the end of the line she was standing in. Jess must have arrived. She kept her eyes fixed ahead, determined not to turn around again. And then she felt something being pressed into her hand by the girl behind her. It was a tightly folded square of yellow paper, with her name on the front inside a border of hearts and flowers. Hiding from Miss Gibson's view behind Nikki's back, she unfolded it quickly, wondering what she'd find.

Dear Sunny

I'm really sorry I was so mean yesterday. Can we be friends again? I tried to ring you at home yesterday, but your phone was engaged all the time. I couldn't sleep last night, I felt so bad. It's just that Mum's been giving me all this hassle about not working hard enough at school ('Why can't you be more like Sunny? blah blah blah'), and I thought you were getting at me too.

Do you forgive me? Please say yes and put
me out of my misery!
Lots of love
Your sad friend Jess
XXXXX

Jess

Immediately, Sunny felt a huge wave of relief
rushing over her. Of course she forgave Jess!
How could she ever have doubted her in the first
place? Snatching a quick peep over her shoulder,
she saw Jess's freckled face looking anxiously back
and gave her the biggest, friendliest smile she could
manage, and a thumbs-up sign. There was no time
for anything else, because the doors had been
opened and everyone was flooding into school.
Well, at least *that* problem's sorted, Sunny thought
to herself, her heart lifting as she went inside.

She waited for Jess to arrive in their classroom,
and hurried over to meet her as soon as she
appeared. 'I'm sorry too,' she said, after they'd
hugged each other tightly. 'It was all my fault in
the first place. I was in a bad mood with Anisha,
but I shouldn't have taken it out on you.'

'Well, let's not have another argument about

whose fault it was,' Jess smiled, her eyes shining. 'I don't want us ever to fall out like that again! Promise?'

'I promise!' Sunny said, giving her another hug for good measure. 'But listen, Gingernut – I've got something amazing to tell everyone. The most incredible thing's happened!'

'Settle down, please, everyone!' Miss Gibson called. 'Time for some hush now.'

'We'll all have to meet up at break,' Sunny whispered. 'By the dustbins. You're not going to believe this!'

Jess, Michelle, Caz, Lauren and Nikki stared at Sunny in complete silence for a couple of seconds. They'd gathered together at their secret hiding place behind the kitchens, where they always went when there was anything important to discuss. Sunny had just told everyone she'd on first prize in that competition they'd all forgotten about, but the news seemed to be taking a little while to sink in. And then suddenly they started hugging Sunny and each other and dancing around for joy, all jabbering and shrieking at the same time.

'That's incredible!' 'You've got to be kidding!' 'Are we really going to have our pictures in the magazine?' 'Sunny, you are such a genius!' 'I knew it! Didn't I say all along you'd win?'

'Just a minute, though!' Sunny shouted above the din. Now came the really difficult part. 'There *is* one problem – something we'll have to decide between us.'

'What's to decide?' Nikki said, pink with excitement. 'We're all going to London! We're going to be famous!'

'Well, that's just it,' Sunny said, taking the *Girlgroove* letter out of her pocket. 'Read this. It's not quite as simple as that.'

Michelle grabbed the letter and the others crowded round to look over her shoulder while she read it out.

'Congratulations! . . . top prize . . . taken by limousine to a photo studio in London . . .'

'A limo!' Jess breathed. 'We're actually going to ride in one of those long stretch jobbies!' And she staggered against the wall, pretending to faint.

'. . . makeovers with our fashion and beauty team . . . modelling a selection of party clothes for a photo shoot . . .' Michelle read on, her eyes widening at the delights in store.

'There you are, Miche,' Caz said, squeezing her waist. 'Modelling! Your dream come true.'

'. . . meal in the Jungle Grill . . .' Michelle read on, her voice rising to a crescendo of joy as she finished, '. . . and an overnight stay in the luxury Burlington House Hotel!'

'Yes, I know all that,' Sunny sighed. 'But look, go back to the first sentence. Who is the prize for?'

Michelle focused on the piece of paper in her hand again. 'For you, four friends and a chaperone who must be over eighteen,' she read aloud. 'What's a chaperone?'

'Somebody who'll keep an eye on us,' Sunny replied automatically.

'Well?' Michelle said. 'Is that the problem?'

Lauren was the first to realise. 'No, it's not,' she said slowly, shaking her mop of dark curls. 'It's the "four friends" part, isn't it?'

Everyone fell silent as they finally understood what Sunny had been going on about. 'Exactly,' she said grimly. 'One of you five is going to have to miss out. Any volunteers?'

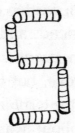

'It's obvious,' Caz said, her face pale but determined. 'I should be the one to stay behind. You've all been friends for ages and I've only just come on the scene. You lot must go – as long as you promise to tell me every single detail when you come back!'

'But that's not fair!' Sunny said. 'There wouldn't be any prize at all if it wasn't for you! It was your party I wrote about, after all.'

'Besides, you're one of us,' Lauren added, 'even if we haven't known you that long. We couldn't leave you out – it wouldn't be right!'

'Thanks!' Caz said, blushing now but looking pleased all the same. 'Someone's got to miss out, though, haven't they? Like Sunny says.'

'Oh, this is so difficult!' Sunny groaned, taking

the letter back from Michelle and reading it over again. There it was, written clearly in black and white: 'you, *four* friends and a chaperone . . .'

She hadn't even begun to consider who to invite as a chaperone, but that could wait. As soon as she'd read the terrible number – four – all she could think about was how on earth to choose which one of her friends to leave behind. It seemed so unfair, but what else could she do? She could hardly ring up Anna Nicholson and say, 'Thanks very much for giving me this prize but, by the way, please can I bring five friends?' It would sound so ungrateful. She didn't want the magazine to think she was a troublemaker, right from the start. They might decide to give first prize to someone else.

'I feel as though I ought to give up my place,' Jess said miserably. 'Especially after the row we had yesterday. But the thing is, Sunny, I *really* want to go. I've never been in a limo or a luxury hotel, and I probably won't get another chance. If you tell me I can't come, that's different. I can't bring myself to offer, though, just to be noble.'

'Nor me,' Michelle said. 'I know exactly what

Jess means. This is about the
most exciting thing that's ever
happened to us, isn't it?
Imagine seeing our pictures
in *Girlgroove*! If I *was* going to
try and become a model –
I'm not saying that I am,
though – I could put
some of the shots in

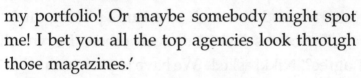

my portfolio! Or maybe somebody might spot
me! I bet you all the top agencies look through
those magazines.'

Thinking it over, Sunny realised it would be
impossible for her to decide who should miss
out. One of her friends was bound to end up
feeling hurt and rejected. 'Look, we'll have to
come up with some way of settling this by
chance,' she said, 'so that it's not personal. Some
kind of act of fate.'

'Like tossing a coin, you mean?' Lauren asked,
and Sunny nodded.

'Perhaps we could draw straws,' Jess suggested. 'I saw that in a film once. One of the
straws is shorter and the person who picks it has

to die, or go first down the escape tunnel – or stay at home while their friends have an amazing time without them.'

'We don't have any straws, though,' Michelle objected.

'Well, we can use something else,' Sunny said. She took the *Girlgroove* envelope out of her pocket and waved it in the air. 'What if I tear this envelope into five strips, make one of them shorter, and you each take turns picking one?'

The others looked at each other. 'Do we all agree?' Nikki asked. 'We have to stick with whatever happens, no matter who picks the short strip?'

'It seems so unfair, though!' Michelle wailed. 'Anyone could get it.'

'You mean *you* could,' Jess muttered under her breath.

'That's the whole point!' Caz said. 'This way, Sunny doesn't have to choose.'

'And no one has any better ideas, do they?' Lauren asked. 'Come on, I vote we go ahead. Hands in the middle, press on three.'

They each put one hand into the centre to make a star, and waited for Michelle. Eventually, she nodded. 'OK', she said grudgingly, reaching in to lay her hand on top of the others. 'I suppose so. Let's get it over with, then.'

Sunny crouched down, turning her back on the others. Carefully, she folded the envelope and then tore it into five strips, one of which she tore in half across the middle. Arranging them in her right hand so that only the first few centimetres of each strip showed and they all looked identical, she held her fist out to the others and waited for someone to choose.

Jess went first. Her hand hovered over Sunny's for a few seconds, then she shrugged and plumped for the middle paper strip. 'Yes!' she shouted, waving it in the air for everyone to see. 'That's a long one, isn't it? I'm in!'

Sunny rearranged the four remaining strips and held her hand out again. 'Who's next?'

'Me!' Michelle said promptly. 'I've just worked out that if you go first, there's more chance of picking a long one.'

'Yes, but if you wait till the end, someone else'll probably take the short straw before you,' Nikki said. 'That's my strategy, anyway.'

Michelle hesitated for a moment, biting her lip, but then she went ahead. After choosing her piece of paper, she hid it for a moment to examine in secret before letting out her breath with a whoosh of relief. 'It's long,' she said thankfully, showing the strip around.

That only left Caz, Lauren and Nikki.

'Me next,' Caz and Lauren said, at exactly the same time, and then smiled nervously at each other.

'It's OK, you can go,' Caz told Lauren, nodding at the three strips left in Sunny's hand.

Lauren picked the middle one – and then gasped in disbelief, staring at it. Everyone could immediately see that the scrap of paper in her fingers was half the size of Jess and Michelle's.

'Oh, Laurie!' Caz said, rubbing her back. 'I'm so sorry.'

The others immediately crowded round to sympathise too. Lauren was hugged, and patted, and clucked over, and promised all kinds of favours to make up for what she'd be missing.

'It's OK,' she said, quickly wiping her eyes with the back of her hand. 'I don't really mind.'

But everyone could see that, of course, she *did* mind – very much.

Sunny found the rest of the week very hard, seeing Lauren's miserable face and knowing she was partly to blame. She couldn't help but feel excited at the thought of what was in store the weekend after next – who wouldn't be? – but they all tried not to talk about it whenever Lauren was around. And yet, clamming up as soon as she appeared didn't seem right either. It was as though they were deliberately leaving her out. Sunny felt like asking one of the others to offer Lauren their place. But that would only be swapping one unhappy person for another, wouldn't it? There didn't seem any way round the situation.

To make matters worse, Sunny's win was now common knowledge throughout the school. Everyone in her class got to hear of it first, and the news spread like wildfire. For a few days Sunny was the centre of attention. At breaktimes she found herself surrounded by a buzzing group of girls, all eager to hear exactly what she would be doing in London and who was going with her.

Then Miss Gibson told Mr Hall, the Head Teacher, about Sunny's prize-winning essay and just about the most embarrassing thing in the world happened – she had to go up to the front in Friday morning assembly while the whole school gave her a round of applause.

Standing there, feeling horribly self-conscious, she tried not to focus on the sea of curious faces in front of her. Although her friends were smiling, several nasty looks were coming her way, too. Most people had seemed genuinely pleased when they heard about her win, but she could tell that a few of the girls were dead jealous. There'd been some spiteful whispering, and Melissa Wilkins was telling everyone that Sunny's dad had bribed the magazine to give her the top prize. No one believed anything Melissa said, but still, the rumours had begun to fly around.

I'll be glad when everything's back to normal, Sunny thought to herself as she waited for her mum to pick her up after school on Friday. Still, at least all the practical arrangements had been decided by now. At first, Sunny's mother had wanted to go along as the chaperone. Trying not to hurt her feelings, Sunny had eventually managed to persuade her to stay at home with Anisha, though. Her mum was so out of touch! She had no idea about fashion and she didn't really approve of make-up, either – Sunny could just about get away with nail varnish and glitter if she was going to a party, but no more. She could just imagine her mother popping up at the photo shoot and telling them all to wash their faces and change out of those ridiculous clothes. It would be *sooo* embarrassing!

Finally, they'd settled on a compromise. Michelle's mother, Yvonne, had offered to take the girls. She was quite young and trendy – more like an older sister, really – and she worked as a beauty therapist in a big department store, so she wasn't likely to be shocked at the sight of make-up. She often worked on Saturdays, but she'd been doing loads of overtime recently and her boss had agreed to give her the day off.

'Don't worry, Shaila,' she'd assured Sunny's mum. 'I'll take good care of them, I promise.'

Now the only thing left to be done was for Sunny to make sure everyone's parents had signed the consent forms, giving permission for their daughters to stay in London under the care of *Girlgroove* magazine. Everything else was settled. The five of them were going, and they'd just have to be extra nice to Lauren, to make up for her missing out. Maybe they could take round a funny video and a bucket of popcorn at the weekend. At least it would show they were thinking about her.

Sunny was just checking her own consent form on Saturday morning – and re-reading Anna Nicholson's letter for the fiftieth time – when Sachin called upstairs to say there was a phone call for her. It was Jess.

'Hiya!' Sunny burbled into the receiver. 'What's up? How did the football go? Are we going to meet up this afternoon?'

50

'Can you come to my house?' Jess asked abruptly. 'As soon as possible.'

Sunny felt her heart sink. She could tell from Jess's voice that something was wrong. 'But we're just about to have lunch,' she stammered. 'What's the matter? Are you OK?'

'I'm fine,' Jess said. 'It's Michelle. Something terrible's happened – I can't tell you over the phone, but she's here with me now. Come as quickly as you can!'

By the time Sunny appeared at Jess's house –
having bolted down her lunch and cycled over as
fast as she possibly could – everyone else was
already there. Jess opened the front door and
took Sunny straight up to her room. Michelle
was slumped on the bed, her eyes pink and
swollen from crying and a tissue in her hand.
She looked awful! Caz was next to Michelle with
one arm round her shoulder, while Lauren sat on
the floor with her back against the bed. Nikki
had bagged the revolving desk chair and was
slowly spinning back and forth in a semi-circle.

'Miche! What's happened?' Sunny gasped,
rushing over to the bed and sitting on her other
side. 'Tell me!'

Michelle drew in a long shuddering breath.

'My aunt's died,' she said, fiddling with the tissue. 'Well, my great-aunt. Gran's sister.' And more tears began to well up in her eyes.

'Oh, I'm so sorry!' Sunny said sympathetically, patting her knee and feeling rather helpless. 'Were you very close?'

'No, I only met her once!' Michelle snapped. 'That's not why I'm crying. She was a mean old bat! Always going on about how Mum had let everyone down by having me without being married.'

'So what's the problem?' Sunny asked, baffled. 'Is your mum very upset?'

'No! She isn't!' Michelle said, throwing off Caz's arm and jumping up from the bed. She started to pace angrily up and down the room, kicking aside one of Jess's trainers and her school sweatshirt, which was lying crumpled on the floor. 'That's what makes it so unfair! She's being a complete hyp— Oh, what's the word – when you do

53

something you don't believe in? Sounds a bit like "hypnotist"?'

'Hypocrite?' Sunny suggested, and Michelle nodded her head vehemently. 'That's it! She's a big fat hypocrite!'

Sunny had never heard Michelle speak like that before – she and her mum were really close and they hardly ever argued about anything. Whatever could Yvonne have done to make her daughter so upset?

Caz solved the mystery. 'The funeral's next Saturday,' she explained. 'Michelle's mum says she's got to go.'

'Oh, I *see*,' Sunny said, as understanding dawned. Out of all of them, Michelle was the one who was probably most looking forward to being photographed and appearing in the magazine. No wonder she was in such a state!

'Mum says all the family's going to be there,' Michelle went on miserably, looking out of the window. 'Her cousins and everyone. She wants to show them I haven't turned out so badly after all. She says she can't bear to imagine their faces

54

if they find out I've gone to a photo shoot instead of paying Aunt Lily my respects!'

Nobody quite knew what to say – not even Jess, who was hardly ever stuck for words. It was a catastrophe.

'Still, looking on the bright side – if you don't come, then Lauren can take your place,' Nikki said, revolving slowly in the chair.

'Nikki!' Caz exclaimed, shocked. 'How can you be so heartless?'

Michelle dissolved in a fresh wave of tears and sat back down on the bed to be comforted.

'It's OK, Miche,' Lauren said, patting her leg. 'If you can't go, then I won't either.'

'And for goodness' sake, Niks, stop doing that!' Jess exclaimed, her auburn hair swinging as she held the arms of the chair so Nikki had to stop turning it. 'You're really getting on my nerves!'

'Well, sor-ree!' Nikki said, her face a few centimetres away from Jess's. 'But you've got to admit, it does seem crazy for Lauren to miss out when there's a spare ticket.'

'I suppose so,' Jess said, letting go of the chair.

And then another thought occurred to her. 'Hang on! There'll be *two* spare tickets, won't there? If Michelle's mum isn't coming, we'll need to find another chaperone.'

'That's true,' Sunny groaned. 'Oh, I hope this doesn't mean my mum will start saying she wants to take us again. I only just managed to talk her out of it the last time!'

'But who else can we find to come along?' Nikki said. 'We'll have to have somebody's mother as a chaperone, won't we? It's a pity – Michelle's mum would have been ideal.'

'Stop it!' Michelle wailed, lifting her tear-stained face and staring accusingly at her friends. 'Stop going on about mothers and chaperones! What about *me*? What am *I* meant to do?'

There was silence for a few seconds. 'Oh, this is awful,' Sunny sighed, twisting her fingers together agitatedly. 'I'm beginning to wish I'd never won this competition! It's just making everybody miserable! First Lauren, and now Michelle. Maybe I should ring *Girlgroove* and say I'd sooner swap with someone who's a runner-up.'

'But then we'll *all* miss out,' Jess objected, 'and you'll end up with *five* miserable friends.'

'We'll all be equally miserable, though, won't we?' Sunny said. 'Except for me, cos I'll have my Glitterbug vouchers – but that's fair enough, as I won in the first place. It won't be a case of everyone having fun except for one person. It's been killing me seeing Lauren so sad all this week. And don't start saying you don't mind again, Laurie – it's not exactly convincing.'

Lauren smiled up at her. Sunny jumped to her feet, coming to a conclusion at last. 'I'm just going to have to ask Anna Nicholson if I can bring five people with me,' she declared. 'If she says that's impossible, well then, I'd sooner be a runner-up. This prize might be amazing, but it's not worth losing friends over.'

'Oh, Sunny – that is so sweet,' Lauren said, scrambling up to hug her, and Caz joined in too.

'All for one, and one for all!' Nikki cried, taking a crafty spin in her chair while no one was looking.

'That's all very well, but I'm still stuck with going to this funeral, aren't I?' Michelle said, blowing her nose and chucking yet another tissue in the bin. 'What's the point of you insisting on taking five friends when one of them can't come anyway?'

'Perhaps we can sort that out,' Sunny said. 'Look, have you talked everything over with your mum? Does she know exactly why you're so upset?'

Michelle shook her head. 'There wasn't time. Mum only told me about the funeral when she picked me up from drama today, and it was her lunch hour so we couldn't really discuss it. She had to drop me here and go straight back to work.'

Living so close to each other, Michelle and Jess usually spent Saturdays together when Michelle's mum Yvonne had to work. Yvonne would give Jess's mum Trish a facial or a massage in return, and Trish – who was a music teacher – often helped Michelle with her singing. It was an arrangement which suited everyone.

58

'Besides,' Michelle went on, 'we ended up having this huge row in the car and I was too upset to talk properly.'

'Well, that's what you need to do,' Sunny told her. 'You've got to calm down and explain everything. Tell your mum how much this London trip means to you! You might be able to win her round if you don't lose your temper.'

'Perhaps you could offer to meet your rellies another time?' Caz suggested.

Michelle thought it over. 'It's worth a try, I suppose,' she said eventually. 'I've got nothing to lose, have I?'

'Exactly!' Sunny beamed, feeling happier than she had done all week. She'd straightened out her priorities now. As long as the six of them tackled their problems together, everything would turn out for the best in the end. She was sure of it!

Sunny frowned at the computer screen. It was Saturday evening and she was finding that hitting on exactly the right tone for her e-mail to Anna Nicholson wasn't easy. She had to show how grateful she was for being given this prize in the first place, without sounding like a real crawler. And she had to let Anna know how impossible it had been to choose who to leave out, without coming across like a pathetic wimp who couldn't go anywhere without her friends.

Eventually, though, she managed to finish a note that she was reasonably happy with. She read it through one last time, then shrugged and clicked the 'Send' button. Anna would receive the message as soon as she got into the office on Monday morning – all Sunny could do now was wait for a reply. She had to go out all day on Sunday, too (visiting another set of relatives so that her mother could tell them how wonderful she was!), so she had no idea whether Michelle had managed to talk her mother round.

First thing on Monday morning, though, Michelle came rushing up to her in the playground, with Caz, Jess and Lauren in tow.

'I did it!' she said, her eyes sparkling. 'You were dead right, Sunny – we had a proper talk about the whole thing and Mum agreed in the end. She says I don't have to go to the funeral!'

'Brilliant!' Sunny cried, giving her a high five. 'How did you manage to persuade her?'

'Well, I reminded Mum of all the horrible things Aunt Lily used to say about us,' Michelle grinned. 'How single mothers were a drain on society and that kind of rubbish. She probably wouldn't have wanted us at her funeral anyway! Mum agreed with that, but she said we ought to be there because it was a family occasion and we should support Gran. So then *I* said, why didn't we ring Gran up and ask her how she felt about it? And *Gran* said she couldn't see the point in me coming if I was going to be miserable the whole time. And *she* didn't care what the stuffy cousins thought about it, so neither should we.'

'Yay! Good for her,' Jess said, jumping up and down in a victory dance. 'Grannies rule!'

'So, sorry, Lauren, but it looks like I'm in,' Michelle said.

'Well, listen – I've e-mailed Anna Nicholson about the whole thing,' Sunny told them. 'I explained how I'd sooner not have the top prize if you couldn't all come.'

'Let's just hope Anna says yes, then,' Caz said. 'But tell us, Miche – is your mother still going to the funeral, even if you're not?'

'Yes, she is,' Michelle said. 'I was going to mention that. She says sorry, but she can't take us to London on Saturday – if we *are* going, that is. We'll have to find another chaperone.'

'I've been thinking about that, as it happens,' Caz said, looking round to make sure she had everyone's attention. 'What about Natalie, my stepsister? I bet she'd like to come and she's closer to our age than somebody's mum, so she'd be more of a laugh.'

'She's not eighteen, though, is she?' Lauren asked.

'Yeah, she is,' Caz assured her. 'It was her birthday a couple of weeks ago.'

Sunny considered the idea. Natalie looked on the weird side, with her heavy make-up and spiky hair, but they'd all got to know her at Caz's party and found out that she wasn't half so scary underneath. She didn't show off or make a big deal about being older and more responsible than they were, and she didn't treat them like irritating little children. Going with Natalie would be a hundred times better than going with her mother. But would her parents agree? Would they trust Natalie to take care of their darling daughter? And what would all the other mums and dads think about it?

'Let's wait and see what Anna says,' Sunny decided. 'If she agrees that we can all come, then perhaps you could ask Natalie, Caz, and see if she'd be prepared to take us.'

'I'm sure she will,' Caz said. 'She wants to work on a magazine, and it'd be a chance for her to make some contacts. Maybe she could go round and talk to your parents, too, so that they can see how responsible she is. I'll get her to tone down the make-up and take out her nose stud first.'

'Mum's not going to mind about that,' Sunny said, smiling. 'She's got one herself, remember?'

Somehow, the idea of Natalie and Sunny's mum having *anything* in common made them all burst out laughing. So now everything depends on what Anna Nicholson says, Sunny thought, watching her friends' happy faces. Oh, I hope she lets us all come! She just *has* to!

As soon as school was over that day and Sunny was back home, she raced upstairs to the loft and logged on to the Internet. Anna Nicholson had replied! Sunny clicked on the message sitting in her Inbox, hardly daring to think what it might say. She ran her eyes down the screen. After a bit of blathering on about the budget for this prize, which was the most lavish one the magazine had ever given, and how much they'd all loved Sunny's entry and of course she mustn't consider swapping with anyone else – Anna finally said yes! Sunny *could* bring five of her friends, as long as they didn't mind squashing up in the hotel and didn't all pick the most expensive thing on the menu at the Jungle Grill. The limo would be turning up at her house, 9.30 sharp on Saturday morning, to pick them up – all six of them, plus their chaperone!

Sunny let out a whoop of joy and punched the air, before reading Anna's message through a couple more times to make absolutely sure she'd got it right. She smiled to herself and shook her head. After all the hassle and heartache they'd gone through, all it had taken to solve the problem was a simple note! Why hadn't she tried that in the first place? But, on the other hand, at least she'd been able to show Anna that they hadn't taken anything for granted, that they'd tried to work things out themselves first. Perhaps if they'd asked her straight away, she wouldn't have said yes.

Sunny ran downstairs again and picked up the phone. She had some news for Lauren that was going to make her a lot happier than any video fest could have done!

It seemed to take for ever for that week to pass, but at long last Saturday morning arrived. Sunny

was up at six, packing
and re-packing her
overnight bag and
trying to decide
what to wear. The night
before, her mother had given
her the most amazing top to
wear for the evening – white, with
a sparkly border of pearls and silver
beads around the hem, the V-neck and the edge
of the long sleeves. It came from the new shop in
the precinct, which was so amazingly trendy
Sunny couldn't imagine her mother even knowing it was there, let alone going inside. She
eventually decided to travel in a pair of dark
jeans with a cool snakeskin belt and her current
favourite T-shirt – white, sprinkled with rain-
bow-coloured dots – as the leopard-print top
made her look like she was trying too hard.

Caz and Lauren were the first to arrive, around
eight-thirty, with Natalie close behind. The two of
them were hopping up and down with excitement, bulging overnight bags slung over their
shoulders, and even Natalie was smiling.

'Sunneee! Isn't this amazing?' Caz shrieked as soon as Sunny opened the door, and Lauren was grinning from ear to ear. They were both looking good – Caz in a stripy blue T-shirt and flares, Lauren in embroidered jeans and a tie-dye pink and purple top. Although it was a sunny day, Natalie wore a dark grey pinstripe shirt under her leather jacket, together with black drainpipe jeans and a pair of spike-heeled ankle boots. She'd gone easy on the make-up, though, and it was surprising how pretty she looked.

Sunny's mother took both Natalie's hands and folded them in her own. 'Now you will look after the girls, won't you?' she said. 'You won't lose them in Carnaby Street or Soho or anywhere like that?'

'It's OK, Mrs Kumar – no worries,' Natalie said in her deep voice. 'I'll stay with them all the time. And I'm taking my mobile phone, so we can keep in touch.' She patted the pocket of

67

her leather jacket. 'I gave you my number, didn't I?'

'Don't fuss, Mum!' Sunny said. 'The limo's taking us straight to the photographer's studios, and then we go directly to the restaurant and the hotel from there. We won't have a chance to get lost!'

Jess and Michelle were next on the doorstep, ten minutes later. 'I hardly slept at all last night, I was so excited!' Jess said, bursting into the hall with a rucksack on her back. 'D'you think these trousers are OK? Not too boring, are they?' She was dressed in plain black jeans with a white T-shirt and a black gilet.

'You look great!' Sunny had assured her. 'Really smart.'

'Well, this is a posh hotel we're going to,' Michelle had said, following Jess into the house. She was wearing a silky, Chinese-print skirt and pulling a zip-up suitcase on wheels. 'You never know, they might have a dress code.'

'Miche! We're only staying overnight!' Sunny protested. 'Looks like you've packed enough stuff for a month!'

'Wait till you see what I've got!' Michelle said, beaming. 'You know Mum's so friendly with the fashion buyer at her store? Well, she let her borrow a whole load of samples from their new range, so I could choose something for tonight. I couldn't decide, of course – so I've brought the lot!'

'Oh, can I have a look?' Jess asked straight away. 'I forgot to bring my red boob tube – talk about stupid!'

'No way!' Michelle replied promptly. 'Sorry, Jess, but I can only wear the one outfit Mum's buying me. Everything else has to go back to the shop on Monday – unworn. Mum'd kill me if she knew I'd even brought it with me! I just have to make sure everything's back in the bags before she comes home from the funeral tomorrow.'

They went into the front room to wait for Nikki and keep an eye out in case the limo was early. To begin with, Sunny wasn't that worried that Nikki hadn't arrived, but as the minutes ticked by, she started to feel nervous. She'd told everyone to be at her house by nine o'clock sharp, and now it was quarter past.

'Oh, where is she?' she grumbled, looking at her watch for the twentieth time. Nikki often cut things fine, but it wasn't like her to be *this* late.

And then there was a ring on the bell. Sunny rushed to the front door and flung it open. Nikki was standing on the mat, bent double with her hands on her hips as she struggled to catch her breath. She was wearing a pale green vest top and a pair of cropped jeans.

'Nikki! Whatever happened to you?' Sunny asked, torn between relief and irritation.

'Dad ran out of petrol,' Nikki gasped, straightening up. Her cheeks were flushed and beads of sweat stood out on her brow. 'Would you believe it? I've run the last couple of kilometres. Just as well I was wearing trainers, eh?' She unslung her rucksack from one shoulder and staggered into the house. '*Ouf!* This bag's killing me!'

Sunny didn't reply. She was gazing past Nikki, wide-eyed, as a shiny white limousine nosed its way slowly down her road like a huge basking shark. Rows of sparkling lights shone like diamonds between the four black-tinted windows along its endless sides.

SUNNY'S DREAM TEAM

The car glided smoothly to a halt outside Sunny's house, and she noticed net curtains twitching across the street as their neighbours tried to see what was going on. Nothing as exciting as this had happened round their way for the last hundred years! And then the driver's door opened and a man in a dark suit with a peaked cap climbed out. He walked down the length of the car, opened the passenger door with a flourish, and smiled at Sunny.

'Miss Kumar?' he asked. 'Are you and your friends ready to go?'

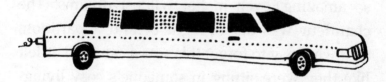

'I could get used to this!' Sunny sighed luxuriously, stretching back against the limousine's white leather seats. 'Better than going on the bus, isn't it?'

She hadn't imagined the limo would be quite so amazing, even in her wildest dreams. The chauffeur was out of sight behind a partition, so it was easy to forget this was a car at all. It felt like they were sitting in someone's cosy living-room! Deep, comfy seats ran around three sides of the limo and a polished wood drinks cabinet stood opposite, stocked with crystal glasses and every kind of soft drink you could imagine. There were two televisions, positioned so everyone in the limo could see a screen. Soft, shaggy grey carpeting covered the floor. The roof over their heads was padded in white leather, with a large mirror set into it so they could check their reflections now and then (every ten seconds, in Michelle's case). It was the most stupendous car Sunny had ever seen.

'Style on wheels,' Natalie agreed, pouring out glasses of lemonade and Coke and handing them round. 'Hey, let's have a toast. Here's to Sunny, for winning such a far-out prize – and for sharing it with us!'

'To Sunny!' everyone repeated, raising their glasses. Nikki's mouthful of Coke went down the wrong way, so she ended up coughing and spluttering and getting most of it up her nose, which sent everyone off in a giggling fit.

Sunny couldn't stop grinning. She felt as though she'd never been so happy. After so much last-minute panic and worry, it was especially wonderful to be sitting here in the lap of luxury with all her friends. And she couldn't wait for the pampering ahead.

'I wonder what the party clothes are going to be like,' she said to Lauren, who was sitting next to her. 'D'you think we can choose what to wear, or will we just have to put on what they tell us?'

'Oh, they must have a selection of stuff,' Lauren said. 'After all, they don't know our exact sizes, do they?'

'My hair doesn't look too greasy, does it?' Caz asked, inspecting a blonde strand. 'I was going to wash it last night but then I thought, if they want to do some fancy styles for our makeovers, it might be better not to have it squeaky clean.'

'This is going to be so cool,' Michelle declared. 'I feel like somebody special already. Look at all those people staring at the car!'

The limo had just pulled up at a traffic light, and everyone nearby was gawping at its tinted windows, hoping to catch a glimpse of some celebrity inside.

'Ha! We can see them, but they can't see us!' Jess crowed, sticking her face right up against the glass and pulling a stupid face. Immediately a teenage boy who'd been peering in started laughing and pointing, nudging his friends. Jess shot back against the seat, her face bright red, and the others burst out laughing.

'They can see you if you practically fall out of the window, dummy!' Nikki told her, as the

74

lights changed and the car pulled smoothly away.

Something about the atmosphere in the limo was so warm and inviting that they were soon all chatting away and swapping secrets as it sped along the motorway. Natalie opened the black padded case on her lap and started putting on her make-up. While she was busy with foundation, eyeliner and mascara, she told them fantastic stories about some of the crazy people at her sixth-form college – including their French teacher, who once rode his motorbike down the corridor and through the main hall. And then Caz plucked up the courage to tell Natalie that she used to be quite scared of her, and Natalie said *she* used to think Caz was a snob because she wouldn't ever talk to her. The next minute, Jess had confessed that she'd been in trouble at home for not working hard enough at school, and Sunny was telling them that it was no joke being thought of as a swot either.

'Half the time, I wish the teachers wouldn't

give me such good marks,' she said. 'It doesn't exactly make me the most popular girl in the class. Still, you've got to admit that being a boffin has paid off this time, hasn't it?'

'Oh, Sunny! Of course it has,' Jess said, squeezing her arm. 'And what's wrong with being clever, anyway? That's why we get on so well: because we're all different.' She raised her glass again. 'Here's to us – the dream team!'

'I need the loo,' Nikki said an hour or so later, shifting about on her white leather seat. 'I wish I hadn't drunk so much Coke.'

'Me too,' Jess said ruefully. 'D'you think we could ask the driver to stop?'

'We should be there soon,' Sunny said, gazing out at the busy streets of central London. 'Anna said the photographer's studio was just behind Oxford Circus.'

She was feeling half excited, half nervous at the prospect of the next part of their adventure. What if none of the clothes fitted them? What if they ended up looking stupid and everyone laughed at their pictures in the magazine? What would Anna

Nicholson be like? She sounded really nice in her e-mails, but you could never tell . . .

Ten minutes later, the limo glided to a halt in a narrow side street. Sunny scrambled forward to open the door, but Michelle held her back. 'No, wait for the driver to do it,' she hissed. 'Act like a celebrity!'

Eventually, the door was opened and the girls piled out, stretching and blinking in the bright daylight.

'There you are,' the chauffeur announced, pointing to a door with a sign on the wall next to it which read 'T P Photography'. 'Have a great session, and I'll be waiting out here to pick you up again at four or thereabouts, when it's over. You can leave your bags in the car.'

'Thanks!' Caz said. 'That was a great trip.'

Sunny had built up a picture of Anna Nicholson: she imagined someone tall and fair, perhaps – definitely trendy. In fact, Anna turned out to be short and bouncy, with lots of wavy brown hair. She looked cool, in her khaki combats and white cotton shirt, but she was the kind of person who made you feel at ease straight away.

'Hi!' she said, flinging open the door to the studio before they'd even had a chance to ring the bell. 'I'm Anna – and you must be Sunny, and her friends! Come on up. We've been looking out for you. What did you think of the limo?'

'Oh, it was amazing!' Sunny said, as they began to climb up a steep flight of stairs. 'This is Natalie, by the way – she's our chaperone.' As Natalie and Anna said hello and started chatting, Sunny noticed Nikki's desperate expression and broke in on their conversation to ask, 'Is there a toilet we could use, d'you think? We've all had loads to drink in the car on the way here . . .'

'Oh, sure!' Anna said, pausing on a half landing to fling open a door. 'In here. Come up to the second floor when you're ready and I'll meet you there. Take as long as you want! No rush.'

'Just in time,' Nikki exclaimed as they were washing their hands afterwards and checking themselves in the mirror. 'I thought I was about to burst!'

Anna was waiting for them on the second-floor landing, holding a mobile phone up to her ear. Something about her expression made

Sunny pause. 'Is anything the matter?' she asked curiously.

'Oh, no, not really,' Anna replied, hurriedly switching off the phone and tucking it back in her top pocket. 'Just a few last-minute hassles. Come and meet Tony, the photographer. We'll need to take a couple of shots before you get all dolled up.'

'Yes!' Michelle whispered excitedly, nudging Sunny in the ribs. 'Now the fun begins!'

Anna led the way into a large room full of photographic equipment and introduced everyone to Tony, a tall man with a beard. He was adjusting a lead which ran from the back of a large camera on a tripod to a computer on a nearby table.

'Wow! Is that a digital plate?' Sunny asked, coming over to inspect the set-up.

'That's right,' Tony replied in a preoccupied tone. 'I take the picture and a few seconds later, it pops up on that computer screen so Anna can take a look. Clever, eh?'

'If you're ready, Tony, I think we should get on with the "before" pics now,' Anna said, chewing her lip.

'If you say so,' he answered, giving her a look which Sunny couldn't quite understand. 'OK, girls, I want you in front of the white backdrop over there. Just relax and give me lots of nice big friendly smiles!'

They gathered together in front of a large white screen with their arms round each other's shoulders. Sunny was in the middle of the group. She tried her best to look happy, but there was a tension in the room which bothered her. Something was definitely wrong – she could feel it. And she could see from the way Natalie was staring round the room that she was puzzled too.

After three or four shots, Tony stopped and looked over at Anna, who was sitting in front of the computer screen. 'Come on – that's plenty,' he told her. 'There's no point in me snapping away just to pass the time.'

'What do you mean?' Sunny asked. 'What's the matter? Something's gone wrong, hasn't it? What's happening?

Anna sighed and buried her head in her arms for a second. 'Louise and Jo haven't turned up,' she said eventually, looking up to meet the girls' anxious eyes. 'Our beauty editor and the stylist. I've got no idea where they are, and Louise doesn't seem to be answering her mobile. I've been expecting them to arrive any second – that's why I didn't want to say anything earlier.'

'I thought there should have been a few more people here,' Natalie said, letting out her breath in a rush. 'This place did seem on the empty side.'

'But can't we begin without them?' Sunny asked. 'Even if we have to wait a little while for the makeovers, surely we could start trying on the clothes we want to wear?'

'I'm really sorry,' Anna said, putting her hand on Sunny's shoulder. 'But the thing is, Louise has all the clothes in the back of her car. There's nothing here for you to wear.'

Sunny stared at her, not sure what to say. She'd spent so long looking forward to this day, imagining how perfect it was going to be. She really couldn't bear it if anything went wrong now!

81

'Don't worry, Sunny,' Jess said determinedly, squeezing her hand. 'They're bound to be here soon, you wait and see.'

'I'll try Louise's number again,' Anna said, punching buttons on her mobile phone. 'This really isn't like her.'

'I have to be out of here by four at the latest, remember?' Tony warned, as Anna held the phone to her ear. 'I only agreed to have this shoot at the weekend as a favour, Anna.'

She nodded, and then held up her hand to signal for silence. 'Louise? Is that you? Thank goodness! Where on earth are you? We're climbing up the wall here!'

Sunny and her friends stared at each other. Michelle had turned very pale, and Lauren's eyes were wide with worry. 'It'll be OK,' Caz whispered reassuringly. 'They've probably just got stuck in traffic somewhere. I'm sure they'll turn up.'

'They'd better,' Nikki said grimly.

Anna's face had suddenly become very serious. She was listening intently to a tinny-sounding voice on the other end of the phone, only interrupting to put in the odd word here and there. Finally she said, 'As long as you're OK, that's the main thing. Don't worry – there's nothing you could have done. We'll talk again soon.' She switched off the phone and looked at the girls for a second without speaking.

'What's happened?' Sunny asked. 'Are they coming?'

Anna sighed. 'I'm so sorry,' she said again. 'It's not looking good. There's been an accident – a car crashed into a lorry just ahead of them. They're not hurt, thank goodness, but their car's been damaged and the police have asked them to stay at the scene to give witness statements. The road's blocked, too. They haven't got a hope of getting here in time, I'm afraid.'

'Well, that's it, then,' Tony said, starting to unplug the camera. 'Looks like the shoot's off.'

'No!' Sunny cried, staring at Anna in shock. 'Not after we've come all this way – in the limo and everything! It can't be!'

'Look, I know this is a disappointment, but it's not the end of the world,' Anna said, trying to cheer the girls up as Tony switched off the lights and began to dismantle the rest of his equipment. 'You can still have a wonderful time going out for a meal and staying at the hotel. And maybe you can come back to the studio some other time. What do you say?'

'But the photo shoot is the main reason we're here!' Sunny protested. 'This trip seems pointless without it. And it's been difficult enough getting everybody together in the first place. I couldn't face going through all that again!'

'Besides, we're all psyched up now,' Jess added. 'We've been really looking forward to having our photos taken. What are we going to do this afternoon instead?'

'Perhaps you could go on a sightseeing tour of London in the limo,' Anna suggested. 'That would be fun, wouldn't it?'

Nobody was convinced.

'Isn't there *anything* we can do to save the shoot?' Caz asked. 'Couldn't we go out and buy some more clothes? There are plenty of shops around here.'

Anna pulled a face. 'Sorry. There's no way I could swing that, even if we had the time,' she said. 'We're nearly over budget as it is, and there simply isn't enough in the kitty to start putting together a whole new wardrobe for you now. We borrow the clothes, you see, in return for advertising them in the magazine – we don't actually pay for them.'

'Wait!' Sunny suddenly spluttered. 'That's it! I've got the answer!' Anna's words had just rung a very loud bell in her head.

'Are you all right?' Anna asked in concern, patting her on the back. 'Here, have a drink of water.'

'We've got plenty of clothes with us!' Sunny explained in a rush. 'They'll be perfect! You don't need—'

Anna interrupted her in mid-flow. 'Listen, I think your clothes are lovely,' she said kindly. 'You all look great. But for a fashion shoot, you have to be wearing the latest gear – stuff that'll be hitting the shops in the next couple of months. And it has to be brand new.'

'But it is!' Michelle squeaked, grabbing Anna's arm and pumping it up and down in her excitement. 'I know what Sunny's going on about!' She swung Anna round so they were face to face and went on urgently, 'I've got a suitcase stuffed full of samples from the department store where my mum works. It's all glitzy party gear – different labels – and it would be *perfect* for the shoot!'

'Are you sure?' Anna said. 'That's unbelievable! Are there really enough clothes for all of you?'

Michelle assured her there were, and Sunny threw in a description of her wicked new top for good measure. That shop in the precinct always had the latest styles months before they reached the high street.

'Come on, let's go and get our cases out of the car,' Jess said, her face alight with enthusiasm. 'Then you can see for yourself.'

'Hang on a minute,' Anna said. 'It's not just a question of clothes. What about hair, and make-up? You'll need to wear some in front of the camera, and I don't have so much as a lipstick with me.'

'No, but I do,' Natalie said. 'I never go any-where without a full set of slap. I'll make the girls up, if you like.'

'And I've got some curling tongs in my suit-case too,' Michelle added.

Anna looked doubtfully at Natalie's black-rimmed eyes and dark, plummy lipstick. 'It's really kind of you to offer,' she began, 'but we tend to go for the natural look at *Girlgroove*. I'm not sure—'

'Don't worry,' Natalie smiled. 'I know the kind of thing you want. Just a trace of blusher for the camera, lipgloss, and maybe a little gold eye-shadow or some glitter here and there? That sound OK?'

'Perfect!' Anna said thankfully. She looked

around at the ring of six eager faces fixed on her own and then raised her voice to ask, 'Well, Tony, what do you think? Should we give this a try?'

'It's your call,' he answered, standing with his hands on his hips. 'I'm happy to go ahead, as long as we're ready to start in the next half hour or so. Otherwise there's not going to be enough time. Sorry, girls, but I can't stay late today – it's my brother's fortieth birthday party, and guess who's taking the photos.'

'Then let's get moving!' Sunny said, making for the door. 'Michelle, we need that case!'

The others followed her, clattering eagerly down the narrow staircase. But when they flung open the door and spilled out on to the pavement, their faces fell. There was no sign of the limo anywhere.

'Now, don't panic,' Anna told them, looking up and down the empty street. 'A car like that can't just vanish into thin air. It has to be around here somewhere.'

'Yes, but where?' Lauren asked desperately. 'If

we don't get hold of the clothes soon, it's going to be too late!'

'The driver said he'd meet us at four, when the shoot was over,' Sunny said. 'D'you think he's parked the car and gone to have lunch?'

'Probably,' Anna replied, gazing up the road. 'Trouble is, there are about a million places to eat round here. I think we'd better split up. Natalie, why don't you take Lauren, Caz and Nikki and head off in that direction. I'll go with Sunny, Jess and Michelle and have a look the other way down the street. We'll meet back here in fifteen minutes at the latest, and hope we've found him by then. OK?'

'Sure,' Natalie said, instantly business-like. 'Come on, you lot!'

Sunny could feel her heart thumping as she hurried along the pavement beside Anna. She couldn't bear to think this brilliant rescue plan might come to nothing just because their luggage had gone walkabout. Jess and Michelle felt the same, too, she could tell; they'd certainly set off at a brisk pace down the road.

In the space of ten minutes or so, they must

have called at at least fifteen cafés, sandwich bars and pubs – but there was no sign of their chauffeur in any of them.

'Oh, where *is* he?' Jess groaned. 'And why did he have to take all our bags with him?'

'I think we'd better be turning back,' Anna said, looking at her watch. 'You never know, perhaps the others have found him.'

'Hang on a minute,' Sunny said, craning into the distance. 'There's a parking sign up ahead. Should we just take a look and see if the limo's there?'

'We could do, I suppose,' Anna said doubtfully. 'One quick look, and then we have to head home.'

Jess, who seemed to have boundless energy, ran on ahead. And then Sunny's heart leapt as she saw her wave frantically back at them from the corner and heard her shout, 'The car's here! We've found it!'

'Now all we have to do is break into the boot,' Anna muttered, as they ran headlong down the street to join her.

As it happened, though, there was no need for

that. Their driver was fast asleep, stretched out on one of the white leather seats in the back. At first it didn't seem as though he was ever going to wake up. But eventually, after they'd shouted and hammered on the window a few times, he opened his eyes and sat up, yawning and stretching. Their luggage was still safely stowed in the boot – including Michelle's precious suitcase – and to save time, the chauffeur even drove them back to the studio.

'See?' Michelle said to Anna, when they were back upstairs and she'd thrown open the lid of her suitcase. 'Aren't these beautiful clothes? Look, they've still got the labels on.'

'Gorgeous,' Anna agreed, picking up a white crop top with a silver star on the front and star-shaped studs all around the hem. 'I wouldn't mind one of these myself. Now, who's going to wear what?'

Michelle picked up a slinky blue dress, the seams topstitched with silver and a fringe around the handkerchief hem. 'This is my favourite – it's what I'd almost decided to ask Mum to buy for me,' she said. 'Does anyone mind if I choose that?'

'You go ahead,' Sunny said, gazing at the layers of shimmery fabric still lying in the suitcase like a hoard of buried treasure. 'There's plenty here for everyone.'

The others had arrived back by now, and they fell on the party clothes like a flock of hungry vultures. Tony showed Natalie into the little dressing room attached to his studio, where she set up her make-up case in front of a large mirror surrounded by lightbulbs. With Michelle's curling tongs and some styling spray that Caz had brought, the beauty salon was complete.

'OK, Michelle,' Natalie said, standing by the door and brandishing a bottle of silver nail varnish. 'Put that dress on and prepare to be transformed!'

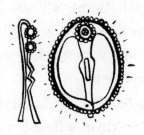

'So, how do I look?' Sunny asked the others, smoothing down her skirt and tweaking the edge of her beaded top. 'Is this OK?'

'You look out of this world,' Jess assured her. 'And your hair is fab!'

Anna loved Sunny's new top and was more than happy for her to model it – particularly as she'd found a silver skirt in Michelle's suitcase which was the perfect match. To finish the outfit off, Sunny had borrowed back the beaded slippers she'd brought Michelle as a present from her summer holiday in India.

'Thank goodness you brought so much gear with you, Miche,' she said thankfully, looking down at them. 'I'm never going to complain about the size of your suitcase again!'

'Just please be careful with these clothes,' Michelle begged them all anxiously. 'Mum doesn't even know we've got them, remember? Put a towel round your neck if you're going to eat or drink anything.'

Ten minutes earlier, a huge tray of sandwiches, fruit and drinks had been delivered to the studio, and they were all about to tuck in. Sunny was suddenly ravenous – it seemed a long while now since she'd eaten breakfast, and a lot had happened since then! But before she could begin eating, Tony waved her over.

'Sunanda, I think we'll have you and Jess now, please,' he said, looking thoughtfully at them both. 'You two match each other very nicely.'

Jess had snaffled the star crop top, which she was wearing with a pair of white satin trousers that had tiny silver studs running up the seams. They were a little too long for her, but Anna had tucked up the bottoms so no one would ever have guessed.

94

Both she and Sunny had a sprinkling of tiny jewels along their cheekbones, and Natalie had braided Jess's auburn hair and finished off the short plaits with silver butterfly clips.

The accessories were thanks to Anna, who had mysteriously disappeared all of a sudden, only to return twenty minutes later with a Glitterbug carrier bag. 'There might not have been enough time to organise new clothes, but accessories aren't a problem,' she'd said, pouring out a sparkling heap of body jewels, hair clips, slides, earrings, rings and bracelets on to the table. 'There's a big branch of Glitterbug round the corner. And they're sponsoring this competition with us, so they don't mind how much stuff we borrow. Get stuck in, everyone! Choose what you like.'

'I don't believe this,' Jess

had sighed, running her fingers through the pile. 'Girl heaven or what?'

Sunny couldn't resist some soft fluffy pom-poms, which Natalie had pinned in her dark hair after she'd piled it up. 'And I'll give you just a hint of eyeliner,' she'd said, skilfully drawing the faintest line around Sunny's eyes. 'Your skin's so good you don't need anything else. There! Perfect.'

Now Sunny and Jess grinned at each other. This was such fun! Following Tony's instructions, they stood back to back and linked arms, turning to the front to smile into the camera. Jess was great at thinking up new poses, and the camera shutter clicked over and over again.

'These pictures are fantastic!' Anna said rapturously from her seat in front of the computer screen.

All too soon, their turn was over and Tony started taking some shots of Michelle on her own. Sunny had felt a little self-conscious to begin with in front of the camera, but Michelle didn't have any worries. She looked so amazing in the blue dress that Sunny felt proud of her, and she could tell Anna was impressed too.

'That girl's a natural,' Anna murmured to Tony when Michelle's session was over, and he nodded his head in agreement.

Mind you, we all look pretty cool, Sunny thought to herself as Lauren emerged from Natalie's improvised beauty salon. She'd chosen a snakeskin print skirt and a fitted silver top, and Natalie had wound a wide silver bandeau through her black curly hair.

Natalie had turned out to be ace at suggesting exactly the right accessory for each outfit, as well as styling everyone's hair beautifully. Caz was wearing a pair of wide-legged black trousers and a top with multi-coloured streamers hanging off the shoulder, and Natalie had picked the perfect jet choker to set it off. Nikki's simple strappy dress was black, shot through with gold thread, and Natalie had teamed it with a narrow gold belt and a handful of gold slides in her wavy blonde hair.

It seemed like only half an hour later when Tony checked his watch and announced, 'OK, girls – that's it. Thanks very much. You've all been great!'

'You certainly have,' Anna said, swivelling round in her chair to smile at them. 'And Natalie – you're a complete star! If you ever fancy a job as a stylist when you finish college, give me a ring.'

'Well, maybe we could talk about that later,' Natalie said, blushing, as she packed away her brushes.

'Sure!' Anna smiled. 'Come on, everyone – you'd better get out of these clothes and give them back to Michelle before she has a nervous breakdown. The limo's waiting and we've got a date at the Jungle Grill!'

'This is such a wicked place,' Sunny said, gazing round the restaurant after she'd spooned up the last of her ice-cream sundae. A couple of huge mechanical elephants stood in one corner, flapping their clockwork ears and trumpeting from time to time. The ceiling was covered in a tangle of creepers, and brightly coloured parrots squawked to each other behind a wire-covered

98

enclosure running along one wall.

Nobody could stop talking about the photo shoot. 'Thank goodness you brought all those clothes, Michelle,' Lauren said, yet again. 'I don't know what we'd have done without them.'

'We'd have had a sightseeing tour round London,' Jess said, grinning cheekily at Anna.

'OK, OK,' she said, throwing up her hands. 'But I couldn't think of anything else to suggest. I wasn't to know you'd brought half the store's new stock along, was I?'

'Do you know what's happened to Louise and Jo?' Sunny asked. 'I feel kind of guilty about that. After all, they were coming to the studio on my account, weren't they? Thank goodness they weren't hurt!'

'I'm sorry they couldn't come, of course,' Caz said. 'But it was great having Natalie as our stylist. I'm going to ask you to do my hair all the time now, Nat.' She twirled the strands Natalie had curled for her with Michelle's tongs.

'Me too,' Sunny agreed, patting her fluffy pom-poms. Although they'd changed back into their own clothes, Anna had let them keep the accessories they'd worn at the shoot, as an extra thank you for coming to the rescue.

'Oh, I'm knackered,' Nikki yawned, and that set everyone else off too.

'Time to hit the Burlington, I think,' Anna smiled, looking at their weary faces. 'I'll come with you to make sure the check-in goes smoothly, and then I'll say goodbye. It's goodbye to the limo too, I'm afraid, but there'll be a taxi coming to pick you up tomorrow morning at nine, to take you to the station. Is that OK?'

'Fine,' Natalie said. 'I've got our train tickets organized.'

'Thanks for everything, Anna,' Sunny said. 'We've had the most wonderful day.'

'But I should be thanking you,' Anna smiled. 'There wouldn't have been anything to show for it without you lot.'

Sunny cupped her head in her hands and closed her eyes. All she could think of now was how wonderful it would be to sink into a soft, comfortable bed and sleep for hours.

Anna paid the bill, and they staggered out to the limo for one final chance to act like celebrities

– although they were almost too tired to play up to the admiring glances thrown their way. It was great to make a dramatic entrance at the swanky Burlington House Hotel, though.

'We'd better make the most of this,' Michelle murmured as they stepped out of the limo and walked up the steps to the hotel's gleaming swing doors. 'It's back to the real world tomorrow!'

I don't mind that, Sunny reflected later, as she washed off her make-up and brushed out her hair in the magnificent marble bathroom leading off their bedroom. It had been the most exciting day she could have imagined – from the moment the limo had turned up outside her house that morning right up to now, when she'd been shown into this wonderful hotel room she was sharing with Michelle – but nobody could live a fantasy life for ever.

Caz, Natalie and Lauren were in the bedroom next door, with Nikki and Jess on the other side. In her heart of hearts, Sunny couldn't help wishing they were all sprawled in a cosy heap on mattresses in the loft room. She felt like going home.

By the time Sunny had brushed her teeth and changed into her PJs, Michelle was already in bed. 'Night, Miche,' she called softly, hopping into the other big double bed.

There was no reply – only a soft, steady breathing.

Sunny smiled, switched off the bedside light and closed her eyes. Well, all my dreams came true today, she thought to herself, just before she drifted off into a deep, delicious sleep. Whatever can I wish for now?

If you enjoyed reading about Sunny
and her party, look out for more
Party Girls books!
And if you'd like to throw a party
like Sunny's, read on . . .

TREAT YOURSELF!

You don't have to win a competition to indulge in some pampering and get a new look! Invite some friends round for a girly sleepover and have some fun spoiling yourselves with top-to-toe beauty treats.

Pillow party invites

These mini pillows make great sleepover invitations. Cut an A4 sheet of plain white paper in half lengthways, then fold it in half across the middle so you have a rectangular-shaped card.

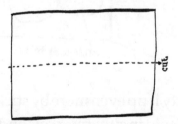

Write your invitation on the front, remembering to mention a time for picking up the next morning and whether you want your guests to bring anything special with them. Decorate the info with felt pens, stampers and stick-on shapes.

Then cover the inside sheet of the card with glue, spreading it right to the edges, and lay a couple of cotton-wool balls on top. Close the card up, pressing the two sides firmly together with the cotton wool between them, and there's your pillow invitation!

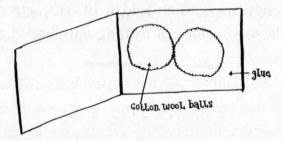

glue

Cotton wool balls

You can pretty it up even more by sticking strips of paper doily (sold in supermarkets and craft shops) around the edge of the pillow to look like lace.

Setting the scene

If your bedroom isn't very big, it might be better to earmark somewhere else to set up the beauty salon. Perhaps your mum wouldn't mind you taking over her room for the evening? Create a luxurious atmosphere with lots of scented candles – but remember, you mustn't *ever* go to sleep with a candle burning. Fragrant oil in a special burner or sprinkled-on pot-pourri smells delicious, too. And there need to be plenty of mirrors, so you can all admire yourselves! Fairy lights around a mirror on the wall will make it look more festive.

Collect together as many towels as you can – the fluffier the better! – plus a couple of hairdryers, some brushes and combs, styling spray, bendy rollers, hair accessories, nail scissors and emery boards. (Ask your friends to bring extra supplies with them if you're running low on anything.) Lastly, don't forget a camera for some before and after pics, or to snap your friends when they're slathered in face masks. Play some relaxing music or find your favourite radio station, and then let the beautifying begin!

Good enough to eat

Raid the kitchen to make these natural beauty treatments:

- Mix a couple of tablespoons of cornmeal to a paste with rosewater. (You can buy rosewater at the chemist's, or make your own by steeping scented rose petals in a cup of water overnight.) Rub it gently over your face, avoiding the delicate area around your eyes, and then rinse off with warm water. This will exfoliate your skin, getting rid of all the dead cells and leaving it soft and smooth.

- To make a nourishing face mask, mash an avocado with a teaspoon of honey. Spread the mixture on to your skin and leave it for ten minutes or so before rinsing off with warm water.

- An egg white, lightly beaten with a teaspoon of rosewater, is excellent for drying out oily skin on the forehead, nose and chin. Apply to your face with a clean make-up brush or some cotton wool. Rinse the mask off when it has dried.

- For super-shiny hair, apply mayonnaise to your wet locks. Wait for ten minutes or so and then shampoo out.

Chill!

While you are waiting for your masks to work their magic, why not relax with a couple of damp tea bags or cucumber slices over your eyes? It's really refreshing!

To give your tootsies a treat, soak them in a bowl of warm water scented with a little essential oil. Dry with a soft towel, rub in some body lotion, then finish off by trimming your toe-nails and giving them a coat of nail varnish.

Give each other foot and shoulder massages, too. Sprinkle a few drops of massage oil or body lotion over your hands and sm-o-o-o-th that skin, squeezing and stroking with gentle circular movements. Feels great, doesn't it?

Crowning glory

Here are some cool new hairstyles to try:

If you have long hair, why not try giving yourself a funky top knot? Gather your hair into a pony-tail on top of your head, securing with a brightly coloured elastic band or beaded scrunchy. Apply a small amount of styling spray or gel to the hair in your ponytail. Then backcomb from the tips down towards the roots – you need to push the comb gently *down* a strand of hair (imagine you're putting the tangles in, rather than brushing them out!). Tease out a couple of tendrils to frame your face, if you like.

To put up mid-length hair, try dividing it into two sections across the middle (imagine a line going from the top of one ear across to the other). Twist the top section around on itself, then secure in place on top of your head with grips or a slide, leaving the ends loose. Twist the second section of hair in the same way, and secure at the back of your head with more grips or a matching slide. Spritz with firm-hold hair spray. (Remember, it's easier to style your hair if you haven't washed it for a couple of days.)

Butterfly clips are great for giving short hair a new look. Spritz first with styling spray or smooth on some gel, then make a parting across the front of your hair to give yourself a fringe. Take small sections of hair, twist each one around at the base and secure with a butterfly clip so that your tiny ponytails stand up. You can backcomb them too (see above), using more spray or wax to keep them in place.

Alternatively, twist your ponytails right to the end and secure them against your head with butterfly clips. Backcomb the very tips of your hair and make sure they stay spiky with styling spray or wax.

Healthy munchies

Give your body a treat on the inside with some yummy things to eat that are good for you, too. These raw veggies are great for dunking into dips: strips of red pepper, carrot and cucumber, mini sweetcorn, sugar snap peas and baby mushrooms.

Try mixing crunchy peanut butter, cream cheese and lemon juice together for a simple homemade dip. Or if there's any avocado left over from your face mask, mash it up with mayonnaise, lemon juice, a little garlic salt and a squirt of tomato ketchup. (These dips taste fab with crisps, too, of course – and with tortilla chips, mini frankfurters, breadsticks, cheese straws and crispy chicken or fish dippers.) If you have a sweet tooth, blend cream cheese and drained, crushed pineapple – serve with a packet of digestive biscuits as a DIY cheesecake.

To make a change from sugary fizzy drinks, provide jugs of sparkling water with slices of lemon and lime floating on top. Peppermint tea is refreshing too, or try an Indian-style milkshake – whizz a banana in the blender with a small carton of natural yoghurt, a teaspoon of honey and half a cup of water.

Finally, you might like to wake your friends up the next morning with fresh-fruit sundaes.

Arrange layers of fruit in pretty bowls or large glasses – try bananas, strawberries, grapes, peaches, or whatever happens to be in season. Serve with some creamy Greek yoghurt for a super healthy breakfast!

hHODDER Another Hodder Children's book

MICHELLE'S BIG BREAK
Party Girls 4

Jennie Walters

Summer's here, and Michelle and her friends are off to a holiday village for a long weekend of non-stop fun. It's going to be great: partying, cycling, swimming and – singing? Yep, singing, Michelle's discovered there's a talent contest coming up, and she's determined to take her favourite position – centre stage!

NIKKI'S TREASURE TRAIL
Party Girls 5

Jennie Walters

Nikki's life is about to change in a big
way. With her family planning to leave
the neighbourhood, she has no idea what
the future holds – and just when she
needs her friends most, they seem to be
playing it cool. If ever she felt like a party
to cheer her up, it's now. But can the
others be bothered to throw one for her?
It doesn't look like it . . .

h HODDER · Another Hodder Children's book

LAUREN'S SPOOKY SLEEPOVER
Party Girls 6

Jennie Walters

Lauren's planned a mega Hallowe'en party, with all the trimmings; ghostly games, pumpkin lanterns, freaky costumes, the lot! When the trick-or-treating finishes, her best friends stay on for a sleepover – and that's when things start getting *really* scary! This is definitely *not* the best night to find yourself all alone in the cold and dark . . .

PARTY GIRLS
Jennie Walters

0 340 79586 7	Caz's Birthday Blues	£3.99	☐
0 340 79587 5	Jess's Disco Disaster	£3.99	☐
0 340 79588 3	Sunny's Dream Team	£3.99	☐
0 340 79589 1	Michelle's Big Break	£3.99	☐
0 340 79590 5	Nikki's Treasure Trail	£3.99	☐
0 340 79591 3	Lauren's Spooky Sleepover	£3.99	☐

All Hodder & Stoughton books are available at your local bookshop or newsagent, or can be ordered direct from the publisher. Just tick the titles you want and fill in the form below. Prices and availability subject to change without notice.

Hodder & Stoughton Books, Cash Sales Department, Bookpoint, 39 Milton Park, Abingdon, OXON, OX14 4TD, UK. E-mail address: orders@bookprint.co.uk. If you have a credit card you may order by telephone – (01235) 400414.

Please enclose a cheque or postal order made payable to Bookpoint Ltd to the value of the cover price and allow the following for postage and packing:
UK & BFPO: £1.00 for the first book, 50p for the second book and 30p for each additional book ordered up to a maximum charge of £3.00.
OVERSEAS & EIRE: £2.00 for the first book, £1.00 for the second book and 50p for each additional book.

Name ....

Address ....

....

....

If you would prefer to pay by credit card, please complete:
Please debit my Visa / Access / Diner's Club / American Express (delete as applicable) card no:

Signature ....

Expiry Date ....

If you would <u>NOT</u> like to receive further information on our products please tick the box. ☐